Hell'**s**

First paperback edition 2023

ISBN   978-1-7381321-6-4   (paperback)
ISBN   978-1-7381322-5-6   (ebook)

hellspress.com

Fairie Tales

Puss in Boots and The Frog Prince

COUNT FATHOM

Dedicated to...

... you, who perceive beauty in a variety of things, yet for whom beauty defies definition. You for whom immorality is identifiable, yet morality is beyond the reach and meaning of your words. You, who suffer the tyranny of appearance over truth.

Dialectic is eclectic, and it's lots of fun. Wind is blowing, lightning showing, storm has just begun. Freezing, seizing, barometric squeezing, shelter everyone. Throes of manic frantic panic, tides oceanic sweep the earth away.

Rant and rave. Coward or brave. Master and slave. Saint or knave. How do we behave to a violent shockwave? Needn't fuss, needn't move, we're sitting in a cave after all. Shadows on the wall tell us of the things that we can't really see at all. Search for your virtue, I tell you, I urge you. Work do, work do, all else you may eschew, for virtue will be the salvation of your soul. What a pleasant goal it is to make oneself whole.

Inspired by Plato

Table of Contents

Preface

Oddities surround us, we pass by them every day. The man that talks to feathered friends and tells us what they say. The girl that makes up consorts round her tea set while she plays. The northern lights, an aardvark, and a shop that sells berets. Changing names of cities , like Mumbai from old Bombay. Too much oddity, however, forewarns of a doomsday.

Too much, I've heard, we have right now, it's climbing up the chart. Much too much contributed, I've more than filled my part. The odd I serve may sting a bit, may taste a little tart, but oddity is what I like, the odd I help impart. Accused I am of wickedness, and far too black a heart. I consider oddity a pleasant niche of modern art.

Here we have a frog that dreams of ruling strict and mean. A cat, as well, improves his lot, and fears not the obscene. In Fairie Tales such happenings are all far too routine. You only think it strange because it's something you've not seen. But such it is, will always be, the laws of Fairie Tales, you'll see, are a lock without a fitting key, and can not be contravened.

Puss in Boots

Better it is to better a friend and draft
from behind to the heights of glory.

"There's nothing like the cavalry, son.
A mounted soldier, properly armoured, is
like a god. I've been blessed to ride in the
vanguard of many a battle, cavalry called
to charge as the opponents footmen are
released. If you're lucky enough not to get
stung by an arrow, by god you mow those
footmen down. You might be surrounded
by three to no effect but your own immense
enjoyment. Give me the cavalry every day
in a battle. An archer? I'd let my kittens be
archers. They won't see real action unless
you get rolled over. By heavens, slaughter-

ing the archers at the end of a good battle is second only to the exhilaration of a mounted charge."

Puss could impress with the pen. Knowing his penchant for embellishment, he made known to good and all that he would not defend his opinions, and reserved well the right to reverse a previous position. Puss would argue that when one engages for the joy of debate, he may well choose to support a losing effort. He will yet pursue his task with enthusiasm, venom and tenacity, all while knowing that the evidence in support of his adversary is formidable, and, in plain truth, unassailable. I, myself, have been influenced by Puss in this regard. Cripplingly disfigured some may say. You may find me waving a flag on a lonely hill for a lost cause that needs defending. If that hill is not yet under assault, well I may claim it to be so anyway. Loudly, belligerently, and to the length mine own satisfaction, I may wail the woe of the long forgotten injustices of yesteryear, of fading fetish fashions of famine fame. Not so Puss.

While he relished and excelled in debate, he was too discerning to allow himself thought the fool for his many and varied interests, and remained reserved. While he could toast a room on occasion, and make merry with his fellows, not once have you seen Puss in a puddle of piss after too many cups. The shame you even thought it so! If he had some interest in you, Puss might catch you on your way out. Or he might bring you a refill just as you needed one. The conversation flowed like a plains river. He could touch on small details of your life, like he knew where you had been last night, of a rendez-vous or triste. He'd know your drink, your childhood pet. Then he'd take what he'd come to get. You'd let it go. Why not? No harm. Charisma. Appeal. He cast a spell, and you fell, quite thoroughly under his charm. Then he's gone.

A legend lives on, and we sing for the love of the song. While this brash little pussy, bigger than most, could take down a mastiff, he often would boast. He bragged that he once sat the throne of the king, and showed off quite proudly his gift of a ring. A ruby set staunchly on top of the gold, of a weight that most pussies just couldn't hold. But we'd better step back, we're ahead of the game. Just how did this pussy acquire his fame? He earned it, I'll tell you with cunning and guile. You'll see if we step back in time for a while.

Not an ordinary pussy, in a litter of but three. He was big. One brother, the younger, swore Puss had eaten the fourth in the womb. That brother died under mysterious circumstances, strangled, by the sewer gate, south of the stone statue. The older lived on, moved west and hitched up with a well wishing witch. But forever a blunder would plunder the value of her best intentioned spells, marring her magic and miring her in misery. The gig fed well and regular despite the worries of the witch. A tickle, he'd said. Hadn't met in years.

Puss was passed to a miller in infancy, and has no recollection of his mother. It was out for himself from day one for poor Puss, for who could he turn to in need? The miller was a fine old fellow, honest and well meaning. The family was a fairie tale, three sons and a dead mother. Thus the need of a cat, the miller thought, to soothe the loss of the mere. Little did he know of cats. And this one was worse than most. For his enemies anyway, or where he might profit.

But let us not sully the kitten for the acts of the cat. Puss, as he was called by the miller, was a perfect pet for the farm. He hunted with odyssean craft. I once saw a herring hop from a river to his paw because he asked it nicely. He kept watch for weakness and exploited where he could. The eldest son was useless, stingy, dangerous when drunk, and Puss long harboured plans of revenge. The middle son worked in his sweat in the sun, to bend to the laws of frère number one. The youngest, the bullied, the smallest third son was the miller's most favoured, but feckless and dumb. Puss stayed close, for when fortune shines, if you are near, you may bask in the reflected glow. Puss needed a tool to carve out his social position in the world. This

favourite frère would fair nicely for Puss
as a stooge in his clever act, worthy of the
stage, and enshrined amongst a pantheon of
fabled legends.

Thinking much of himself, Puss, poised
purposefully on his hind legs, practiced par-
ries and lunges on posts. He was an excellent
boxer in the amateur ranks, scoring well and
much admired, but lacking finishing power.
He was as well versed in the art of conversation. His company was much comment-
ed on in the family, and Puss swelled with
pride. Yet these skills were but a dull grey
when compared to the blinding colour of a
Puss hunt.

Puss would pin flies, mid flight, with a
paw. His patience could wait days for thick
ice to thaw. Intelligent, cunning, nimble,
and quick, Puss could lift eggs with a sleight
of hand trick. A mongoose, a python, a dog,

and a goat. Puss could kill all with a strike to the throat. To hunt was the one thing this Puss would pursue forgoing all profit, a joy, pure and true. When he's on a hunt, you hear what I say, you leave Puss alone, don't you get in his way.

Days are long when you're a talented Puss trapped in the tedium of village life, a prison for the mentally competent. Shall we forgive him his little cruelties? Frere number three, the youngest and weakest and kindest and dumbest, most people around didn't know his name, cause they couldn't care less. It was Herbert. Herbert Miller. Poor Herbert might have his shoelaces cut short one morning, and his sugar replaced with salt the next. His door might be glued shut, or his bed raised a foot in the night. The wet paint in his cap went unnoticed until he took it off to dine. He felt he would die waking one morning and rubbing his eyes with ground chillies sprinkled on his fingers.

Herbert was more suspicious of his brothers than he was of Puss, who cuddled consolingly, convincing Herbert of his friendship and innocence. Herbert shared everything with Puss. Herbert, not clever enough to interpret another's intentions, was led by the nose as if he'd had a bull ring pierced there. Puss would take hold. Fishing was a frequent early morning excursion, and Puss insisted on sending fish to the king on a regular basis in Herbert's name. Herbert would milk the cows upon request. And Herbert would wake well before dawn to play for a spell, were Puss to smack his sleeping face repeatedly. But he might get a swipe across a forearm were he to interrupt Puss in a nap, or, worse yet, a hunt. A hunt which might begin at any moment. "Fuck you,

Herbert," said Puss. Sometimes before the scratch, sometimes after. Herbert's arms were criss-crossed with wounds, hidden under some young man fur.

Often just two little words could restore Puss to Herbert's good graces. Bulge eyed, submissive, maybe even a tear or two, "I'm sorry" was sufficient atonement for one's crimes according to the justice of fine young Herbert. Puss honed his manipulative abilities on these three young men, completely ignoring the miller himself, much to the miller's despair, which was well known to Puss. Henry, the eldest, should not be provoked. He was a real threat. One day, thought Puss. Hobart, the middle son, lacked emotional response, and Puss was denied his feast. Hobart's annoyance was a meagre meal for the troubles Puss took in the preparation and the cook. Herbert was the third bear. Just right. Herbert would lose his emotional marbles at the slightest distress, screaming, often, crying, always, shaking, seizing, spinning, spitting, hyper-ventilating, sitting, wailing, moaning, groan-ing, sobbing, "Good god, child, stop! My head is throbbing."

And then the poor miller died of a heart attack at fifty three, outliving his spouse by a mere seven years. The three brothers were left to weather the storms of life alone. A will was found among the papers, and after reading it, you will begin to appreciate this miller, and regret you have overlooked his good qualities while he was alive. He should have been recognised for his good and noble spirit, listened to and admired. But no! You've lost the opportunity forever, for he has died.

"To my son Henry, the eldest, the

meanest, the drunk, the despotic tyrant, the pirate, the skunk. You, son, will fare well in this world among men. For each man is your brother, at least nine out of ten. To you I give land and title and deed. You deserve to inherit the curse of Nuck's greed."

"Hobart, my friend, my son number two, all means of production I am passing to you. Take all machine knowledge, pro-duction and tool, and apply them for profit with honour and rule. Hobbie, dear son, I wish you the best. Work hard, my Hobbie, and in peace I can rest."

"Herbert, my son, you're third and your worst. You're useless and vain and thin skinned and cursed. A coward, my son, you've been all of your days. The cat can lord over you, so with you he stays. May the cat bring good luck to you, Herbert, at last. I fear you'll go beggar or bugger quite fast."

"In parting, I don't want to stay and chat, I've crafted some boots, I've left on the mat. They're a gift, I've made for Puss, the cat." A great man has parted. And that was that.

You've been introduced properly to some of the party involved in our adventure, and their relative circumstances. For the moment brother number two continued to apply his industrial production at its present location, and allowed Henry a considerable sum in rent. Interesting decisions Hobart might make are not of immediate interest to a story about our hero, Puss. Herbert was fed. Puss was not idle.

Up until this point you might have been persuaded to regard this particular miller living in an otherwise predictable trope of an village environment, where the rest of village life, with its physical and social apparatus, are common, worthy of no further commentary. But you would be wrong, and you shouldn't speculate like that. But I concede you do need a baseline from which to establish any perspective at all. With culture, or normality, is that baseline possible? Or is the landscape too varied to establish one kind of normal. Any relationship is normal in a chaotic system.

Each fairie tale kingdom is unique in itself, though sharing similarities with the others. The narrow path of virtue is beset on all sides by the dangers and seductions and delights of immoral submission. While only one path leads to purity, all the many others are polluted in their own unique way. Vice and evil have many faces. They even hide as virtue in disguise. Walk the moral tightrope, friends, and stop pushing people off. I see you.

Good King Oliver, the fine featured, fine mannered, fine ruling monarch on the Rhine, slips silently into the background, without the pompous flair of your usual king. Honour is his due, as his rule has been mild, and encouraging for the people. While managing affairs of the state responsibly, Oliver had amassed a fortune in the castle store rooms. Trade from all sectors increased, his people were productive, prospects were attractive to investors and the population grew. He policed responsibly, but was perhaps a bit too permissive with the crown's control over the kingdom. There were still lands in which the king's rule reached only with great effort. Nevertheless, by the standards of his peers, King Oliver is well deserving of the Good.

"Time for the daughter to marry," thinks Good King Oliver. "Whom shall

I pick? They're a bunch of poesies in this stock I see before me. They're living in their own self created fairie tales. Can't they see the nightmare! I want my daughter and her husband to understand as they rule, that our kingdom is always three months from collapse in some commodity. Even with storerooms full, our supplies are eaten through by the needs of the state. I am responsible, but I cannot in good conscience operate below a certain fiscal threshold of dignity in medical care, education, and defence. The kingdom operates near that defined line. And that is why trade and commerce run so well. And why does this Comte Herbert persist in sending me fish?", sighs Good King Oliver as a servant displays the latest river big mouth.

"These petalled pansies reek of ambition, on the tips of their toes trying to sniff higher air, and I won't have that around my dinner table each day until the one I die. I'm going out into the land to find a fine common lad that will rule with honour and grace. Millie, come here now, we'll go find you your husband."

Millie came along, like a good little lass, and they all clambered out in the coach.

But let us return to the unfortunate Herbert and his inheritance, now proudly erect on two feet in boots, the sly and cunning Puss of lore's name. Now afield in summer days with no compass to point them towards some purpose or pursuit, much was yet learned by this unusual pair of provocateurs. Among fens and fowls and foals and fillies and fern and gulley and gorge and glen, through meadow past glade in the valley beyond, lives an horrible man by the name of Du Pont. An ogre, a mon-

ster, who stole, fought and killed. A magical
creature, not cunning, but skilled. He could
change in a blink from fat man to thin, he'd
change dark to light in his eyes or his skin.
Much more than that he could do if he
chose. A tail and more fur, or he shrinks and
he grows. An orange or a peach or a dog or a
cat. Du Pont could pretend to be this or be
that. But you mustn't go near this devilish
troll, he's mean and ill tempered and angry
and cold.

A hero was needed to conquer the land.
As it just so happens we have one on hand.
Herbert may enter with Puss at his side, and
their chance for success is impossibly wide.
For fairie tales end in the usual way, but tell
them we must, for they have this to say, "I
am your culture, your home and your lore, I
can speak for you and let me once more."

Herbert lay, forlorn, at the side of a

splashing river, into which he must plunge. Thus he did, stripping free of his final chains and wobbling gingerly over the rocks and into the stream, naked as the girls I see in my dreams. Puss up on the road was conversing with a toad, when a cart and six came through with the king, and daughter too! Now Puss is not a cat to miss an opportune to chat with the higher social class. He could kiss a little ass, ingratiate himself, and then to further profit he may pass. The good graces of the rich can grant your wish if you will just accept the switch from self respect to friendly fish, to entertain and serve as fool so they can laugh until they drool. Puss had a plan quite fast, into which Herbert could be cast.

Puss, that cunning conniver, rushed down to the riverside, gathered up all of Herbert's clothing, Herbert himself still flapping about in the water, and hid them beneath some rocks at the base of a tree. Puss hurries back up to the king's road, straddles centre, arms to heaven, and garnishes with the irresistible charisma and charm, characteristic of our picaresque hero. Black glob eyeballs, puffed and moist, shy the lead two horses to an abrupt halt. Puss can heat a creature's empathy to a melt, which then spills out of their pores. Even horses! Out pop king and daughter, who slip in the leak of their own empathetic drizzle. Our manipulative Puss feigns a panicked, yet somehow quaint and ingratiating, bow.

"My fair and gracious king, Good Oliver, great sir! My stars! My master's in a mess, my king, I'm desperate for a cure. While bathing in the stream, it seems, a thief has come and gone. His clothes, his things, his modesty, he's naked as a fawn. Safe harbour for my lordship, king, I'm on my very knees. A loyal man, the Comte Herbert is, ask anything you please."

"Bring him along and we'll robe him well. Good acts in good faith are hammer to the karmic bell. We'll live king eternal, incarnate in bliss, if we're worthy of the fondle of fair fate's kiss."

Mollie nodded enthusiastically. Puss ran off to fetch Comte Herbert, to tell him he was now a Comte, to bring him to the king, and to introduce him to the princess. Herbert offered little resistance. Having been told his clothes had gone missing, helpless Herbert allowed himself led to the cart of the king, too simple to cover his shame. And what had he to be ashamed of? Millie thought nothing! Along the Comte came.

"Stop that with your hands, Millie! You'll go blind." Yet the King Good Oliver

could empathize with his lustful daughter.
This Comte was unblemished, tall, strong,
young and clean. Herbert was off to a good
start, and Puss was well pleased with the
blush of the princess and the beam of the
king. Herbert was robed in folds of fur, and
seated next to Millie in the cart. The princess
herself covered them both in a blanket, their
hands concealed, not so their delight.

"Follow the path through meadow past
glade in the valley beyond, till you come
to the land they call the Du Pont. A castle
is there, the valley is fine. Let us repay you
with a meal and some wine, Good King let
us host you, make merry and dine." Puss
bowed with grace this time, as if before
the divine.

Then he took off at a pace the king
would rather not match, and left the king
time to consider his catch. This man, this

great ape, this statue of flesh, would his thought and his morals and principles mesh with the wishes and dreams of the Good great King? Would he bow to the throne? Would he kiss the ring? All this and much more did Oliver ponder as he rode with the fish on his hook into yonder.

Puss flew on through valley, past vale, into the land of the Du Pont tale. Puss marched right up to the castle door, and shouted out frankly, in a Puss like roar, "Ogre Du Pont, you smelly fat cow, drag your thick head outside and confront me right now! You've been evicted, I tell you, by order of King! Good Oliver chose me to deliver this thing. You get out of this home and accept what's been done. The king's on his way and you'd better run!"

A rumble, a grunt, a shake and much more brought thunder enclosing quite fast to the door. It opened a crack and out from the black came a giant unwashed and slovenly boar. Seeing the cat after hearing his rant, Du Pont broke out in a merry chant, "Cat, I'll rip you tail to toe and watch the bloody river flow and you will suffer as you go!"

In a miraculous transformation, Du Pont reshaped into a lion, roaring and charging at our Puss. Puss ducked and dodged this way and that, the lion was no match for the guile of the cat. Minutes of chase drained his spirit away and Du Pont dropped, exhausted, into a bushel of hay, panting and muttering throughout his rest, Puss thought now the time might be best.

"No sense in chasing me all through the day. You'll run out of breath and I'll get away. By order of the king, you are to leave. It's all here in this letter you are to receive. Pardon the size, as you see it's quite small.

The king's mouse wrote it, and he's not very tall. I'll put it here on the ground, for read it you must, but the print is terribly small, hardly larger than dust."

Du Pont was quite worn out, and not bright at his best. He would willingly submit to what Puss might suggest. "Shrink down, like a mouse," was the sly cat's request, "then read, and see after about all the rest." Du Pont was quite stupid, I think it fair to say. Puss enjoyed himself. Puss was moulding clay. Du Pont shrunk down small to not more than an ounce, and Puss, on the hunt, made a bloodthirsty pounce! Puss tore him to pieces with razor sharp claws. He devoured that poor ogre, licking clean his fur and paws.

And how did the staff to the castle respond? As you might expect, they were relieved at the overthrow of poor governance, as most of us are. Puss lined them up straight, to give them a fine speech about the philosophy of leadership and his intentions for the castle, which would now and forever more be the domain of Comte Herbert, and furthermore that the Comte had been so, steward of this land, for generations past, and that were they to perform to his satisfaction in the presence of the king, all might be well rewarded for their new found loyalty. Reaching deep, Puss coloured the denouement of his speech with his characteristic charismatic bulge eyed charm , and a few of the maids wet themselves in... tears.

On anon, along rolls the cart of the king, with the ennobled Comte Herbert wedged snugly within. Under the blanket was unheard of pleasure for Herbert, while above his face glowed a cherry red. The king waxed poetic about justice and law, committees and governance, trade and taxation, public health and morals, education as the founding pillar of a successful and mature society, showing he was not in fact a fool at all. Odd, then, his utter infatuation with our Herbert. Or is it? What kind of son in law might Herbert be? Incompetent, certainly, but then there was that cat, who seemed sharp as a tack. Free of ambition, he'd be docile and malleable. Although, on close inspection, Herbert was not the strapping country simpleton the king was hoping for, Herbert was enough of those things to satisfy much the king desired. There was hope for the grandkids, could they be but parted from their parents.

"Herbert, my boy, you're a special catch. You and my daughter make an excellent match. A splendid estate is before us spread, what a dish! Let us enjoy ourselves on the castle's bread, and of course fish! Should we find peace and pleasure within, there may come a day when you may call us kin."

The staff were superb, well pleased was the king. He gratefully bequeathed to Puss a very special ring. It once did grace a bishop, somewhere off in Rome. Solid gold throughout the band and capped by a ruby dome. Herbert was announced right then as Millie's new man wife, causing all sorts of astonishment, annoyance, commotion and strife. That tale will sit on the shelf for today. We have put this Puss on fame's narrow way. For now he will suffer to bid you adieu. This pussy has some issues, at least one or two, that need his attention if all's to go as planned, and what you need is a paw sometimes to direct fate's hand.

The End

The Frog Prince

A hand held suspended next to the stone frame in caution, Prince Tartakower stepped onto the sill of the lonely arched window in the second highest turret in the Palace of Muglac. Poor Polly paused as he looked over the vast lands of his father's estate. Prince Tartakower resolved to take just a little more time, one more day perhaps, before he leapt, and climbed down from the sill.

He felt friction and resistance from all quarters. As a child he had been received wherever he went, coddled and fussed about in good humour. As he slept, fed by the light of the moon, Polly grew to the age when a boy believes himself a man. Now he is greeted coldly and made to feel unwelcome. Whatever endeavour he cares to undertake, whichever corner of the bureaucracy he requires, at his most timid approach they immediately take an offended defensive posture, and are so overwhelmed by the present work that not a sentence can be spared, goodbye now, Prince.

Reform is devilish jinn, and Polly was possessed. He was upsetting to the reliable, and therefore comforting routine. Accusing him of demonic possession was a frightful bit of fun, not just tolerated but encouraged. Polly's supposed alliance with dark forces would one day be codified into a religion by a small confederacy of enterprising young men. an inner circle of capable acolytes who would enforce upon the public with increased hostility and self righteous condemnation Polly's godliness. Soon grow their fortune and influence. But let's not get distracted and put the cart before the horse.

Polly took long melancholy walks in solitude, baring his tormented soul to all the denizens of the woods. "Why have the fates obstructed me? My ideas to nationalize the peach industry, confiscate land from the peach farmers, thereby reducing unwanted competition in the peach market, providing lower prices for all, was laughed at!. Think of the exports!" Prince Polly proposed a purchase of Peruvian pomegranate, exchanged for state owned peaches, a straight trade between nations of product, thereby evading the costs of the financial plumbing along the way, again ridiculed. They snorted when Polly suggested amendments to early childhood curriculum, enhancing a shared cultural identity. Poor Polly posed forlorn, arched his spine, noggin tilted back, wrist to forehead, shivering a deep selfish sigh into sight. Polly fancied himself dramatically gifted.

His father was Magnate Supreme, a position of unquestionable strength and power within the realm, a realm which Prince Polly would one day inherit. He planned to break the land to his will. Discipline would be imposed. They would be better off for it.

"If only they could see the glorious future I have mapped out for them. I see waste and spoil wherever I look, and all that is needed is the fine management of a superior mind. The consensus is the disease! The representation of the people is but a needless irrelevance. Vie! The day he may die!"

Just then, taking shape from the tangled dark itself, came an elderly woman with a weaved wicker basket, covered and slung in the crook of her arm. The dark came with her. A cloud suddenly blighted the sky. A wilt took hold of the leaves as she passed. Polly, mired in his own woe, felt the looming shadow as a reflection of his own sorrowful spirit, a companion to his soul. And perhaps she is. She is Nuck. And she is a bringer of ill omen. Closer now, Polly was overwhelmed, "Egads! Woman! your breath is polluted!"

It was too late. A hoary palm conjured forth from beneath the cover among her wicked wicker wares a pill of purple powder which she pulverized and puffed into poor Prince Polly's visage. Polly wailed in torment as he shrunk like a frightened turtle, within three teary blinks, into an repugnant fat frog the size of a child's foot. The evil, noxious Nuck gripped the frog in her skeletal claws, and poor Prince Polly's body burst out in bubbles between her fingers. Polly was strangled into silence, and feared for his very life.

"You will suffer, you selfish entitled adolescent. The lives of the people are not play things for your amusement or pride. You are punished to live as an odious amphibian until the day you can prove a creature worse than you. I wish you misery!" Nuck arms and legs synchronize astoundingly accurate to the most exquisite trebuchet, Nuck launched the frog Prince East, over valleys and vales and glen and gorge, and rivulet, stream, and creek, plunging Polly plop into a pond at the far edge of an unfriendly neighbouring fiefdom.

Polly's plunge into the pond was an unimaginable perfection, the angle of his entry coinciding exactly with the muddy slope of the pond's shore. Polly's touchdown was gentle, if fast, but even the slight friction sent him somersaulting at tremendous rotational velocity. He skipped across the surface of the pond like a flat stone, pushed a surf in his wake as he slowed, and sunk, dizzy eyed to a degree you or I might only dream of, suddenly into the murky strangling tangled depths of maddening uncertainty.

He was soon escorted, dragged, really, in a humiliating fashion, and no part of his new body was spared the indignity, to the foot of a mount one side of centre, the eye of yin in the yang portion of the concept shaped pond. One enormous, fat bellied frog sat lord above them all. He was Rana, ruler supreme. Polly must pay obeisance by licking his kingly foot. Dragged, belly through the muck, Polly's mouth suffocated in wet mud. Finally pinned to the earth by the feet of three others frogs, chanting their tribal rhythm, Polly submitted and wrapped his tongue in a sock about the foot of King Rana.

"All must submit to the rule of King Rana." He was told repeatedly, as they snatched flies at dawn and dusk, out looking for a girl, or while just sitting your lily pad in the sun. We mustn't dwell on Prince Polly Tartakower's transition to his new frog life, for that new life became old quite quickly. All the tears and moans and self pity still torment our Polly regularly enough, but there is a life to get on with, and that now consisted of some strange habits indeed. Frogs climb all over one another physically, for example. Polly had a toe up the pooper twice already in a fortnite, and seven times in all in his first ten months, when he stopped counting. But clearly much more frequently than he had suffered such as a man.

About that time, yet another miraculous fireball from the heavens plunged ever so perfectly, as had Prince Polly, into the pond. It was of such tremendous density that it was interred a foot into the muddy bed beneath the pond. Rana ordered a platoon of frogs into action. In their zeal to please the leader, safety was ignored, and, sadly, several frogs lost their lives that day in the dig. In the end, the frogs did recover the mysterious object – a marble of solid gold.

The orb was hoisted above the growing crowd of frogs and triumphantly paraded around the mount seven times clockwise, a wild primordial chant frightening the children away from the violent mob. The frogs with the orb of good fortune held before them began to ascend the mount, towards their King. Rana, sat in smug pride as this treasure was presented to him, and there it sits on his right hand side. He would occasionally give it a pat with his forefoot, or a lascivious lick with his rope tongue.

Life in the land of frogs was unbearable. King Rana was as stupid as he was ugly. The conditions of the frogs might easily be improved, as Polly saw it. But were a frog to undertake an independent action, a threatening glance or burp from Rana, and patrols of henchfrogs would advance in bloodlust. King Rana cared for nothing but the preservation of his position, lord above all. Merciless and exactingly consistent, Rana's rule had been unchallenged for generations. Loyal henchfrogs were rewarded generously from amongst the unfailing tribute to the King, and carried out the wishes of their master with a vicious sadistic enthusiasm.

Thus reform was not discussed openly. Pockets of intellectuals might gather under the cover of dark and discuss intricacies of constitutional utopia, or draft grand proclamations from deep within their dens. But it was impossible to escape the watchful eye of Rana, and none had the courage to openly disobey.

Prince Polly Tartakower, now a common frog in a tyrannical pond, was initiated into the inner circles of the antiestablishment within weeks of his arrival, by a surly old academic named Makogonov.

"You won't find me writing papers", spat the old codger with a sour wince, "The few of these that read haven't the spine for action. I've seen thousands popped like balloons under Rana's foot, both my parents, seven siblings, several girlfriends, and a cloud of eggs of my own before they even had the chance to hatch! It's an effective deterrent. Our lives are miserable, our suffering is severe and unnecessary. But Rana knows he can maintain order. If he can do that, then he can take and do what he likes. His henchfrogs are very much the same. You will never succeed in upending a ruler like that. Not from within the pond."

Polly puzzled his predicament. He, too, sought to break the people to his will. Makogonov was reassuring, in a way, that such was possible. But looking at Rana upon his mount, Polly was disgusted at the pitiful life the frogs must lead under such a ruler. What was it that made life worth living? And would he choose to deprive others of that very thing to achieve economic goals? Weren't those economic goals going to bring happiness to the people? But there could be no happiness when authority is enforced in this way. Polly could not puzzle his way out.

While much of the intellectual chatter was high falutin, and enjoyed complicating simple ideas, there were some of sound mind

and proposition. Makogonov was sandpaper
by nature, intentionally provocative, and
misanfrogic to boot. While not entirely ingratiating, Igor was certainly less poisonous
to one's mood.

"Agency. The individual must perceive
agency in himself. The ability to act and better his position. Give him that opportunity.
The road maps must be clear, orderly, timely,
and accessible. With achievable goals, not
too distantly placed, and the encouragement
and support of the state, you will maximize,
amazingly, both productive participation,
and life satisfaction."

Igor was a gem.

"Perhaps a benevolent dictator would
be best. All could adore him, he would rule
wisely and well, the people could be happy and proud of him as the centre of their
collective cultural unity. If we were of better

mettle the next and the next would serve capably in that role of virtuous authority. But we know frogs too well. So instead we must find consensus."

"Yes, it's slow. And imperfect. Must it always harbour tension? Is that tension inevitably fatal? Are all states doomed to fail? Is there a great universal rule of life? Can we learn from our histories? Are there patterns and laws to be discovered? Some governing principle? Can we one day shine a light of intelligence to illuminate the dreaded blackness of the future? Is peril advantageous if overcome?"

Sometimes Igor was a gem. He would become ensnared in the immensity of the unknown, wandering for hours in the darkness before finding solid ground once again. Polly would wander faithfully at his side for these happy hours.

Way down the road, not so very far off, a jay bird died of a whooping cough. Well, he whooped so hard, and he whooped so long, that he whooped his head and his tail right off.

"Mummy, that's disgusting! Tell the maid to take it away this instant! You there! Take that away right now."

The maid, Tess, mothered this child for the first four years of her life, but Alara hadn't bothered to know her name. Tess bowed her head, lifted her skirt, and scurried off to dispose of the horrific mess made by this poor bird.

Alara could be said to be the world's greatest evil. Some entitled little shit with no respect for the immense wealth and power of their position. Nobles of old were granted their fiefdoms at the pleasure of the king, and thus required to provide tax collection and soldiery in times of war. The nobles were stewards of the land, maintaining tradition and integrity, to the extent their abilities allowed. With wealth came responsibility. But how sadly social harmony has collapsed, as the rich reign irresponsibly .

The bird wasn't sick. Tess had told Alara so to relieve her of the horror of the truth. That bird had been shot for sport by Alara's father only moments before. The party of three heard the report, and knew of the master's proclivities. Shooting birds from the roof was among these.

The shot that took the head off our poor jay bird was a one in a million. Grand Pooba Kerem won the bet and collected his money immediately from the briefcase of his compatriot, Lesser Pooba Mirac, in an tributary solicitation to gain favour with the Grand Pooba. Knowing both Kerem's vanity and his excellent marksmanship, Mirac had bet that Kerem could not kill that sick jay bird with one shot. Mirac proceeded to supply his friend with a solid gold bullet. One shot, for sport, for a million. Off popped the top, to Alara's disgust. And thus begins our adventure.

"Maid! You take mother along back to the manor. I'll be along in a moment." Alara frequently expressed herself in command. Her every thought beckoned action somewhere, from someone. Mother and maid made off, and Alara walked the spacious forest path out to the edge of the Red Pond, named in honour of the bloody frog carnage often found thereabouts. The pond was avoided as a cursed place. Alara thought that silly, and round about the edge of the pond she walked in a leisurely stroll, thinking herself wonderful, unlike the ignorant ninny

goats she must suffer, when what did she spy
'pon the mount in the eye but a shiny gold
ball did there lie!

"You there!" Prince Polly was taken
aback. But having become accustomed
somewhat to his lower standing in the social
hierarchy, our proud Prince bowed and
scraped belly, in his froggy way, up to this
demanding titan, and asked if he could be
of service. "Fetch me that gold marble there
out on the mount. Try not to touch it too
much, you filthy lech."

"Pardon me, princess. But that is King
Rana's trophy, his most prized possession,
a symbol of his power over the others. The
frogs would vie with one another to hand
Rana my sorry head. The risk is too great."

"Don't lecture me about some fat froggy
king. Get that treasure right now or I'll pull
you inside out!" Polly took several cautious

hops backwards into the pond, keeping his
eyes above the water line, and shivering in a
healthy fear.

The impertinence of this blasted frog!
Alara was vexed. This beggarly bastard
was squeezing her into negotiation. Seeing
herself tied down over the barrel, Alara,
loathe though she was to do it, considered
the compromises she might make in order to
acquire her prize.

"Look here you! You go fast and get
me that gold. That fat blob won't catch you.
Race his little thug army back here with my
ball, and I'll protect you."

"Princess, if I have your solemn oath,
on your very honour that you will carry me
back to the manor and care for me until my
dying day, then I will be your champion."

Alara quite liked this chivalrous amphibian. He showed spine, and spirit. "We

have an accord, my froggy friend."

Polly turned and stretched into a swim towards the base of the mud mount rising from the eye of the pond, where Rana perched in the pride of his magnificence. Blending into a tribal chant dance in the accepted clockwise manner, Polly surreptitiously began a slow ascent towards the peak. Within a few hops now from the prize, the golden bullet poised protectively under Rana's fanning forefoot, Polly made a maddened dash , and, in an audacious and suicidal surprise, pushed the ball into a roll.. Pandemonium and panic struck throughout the pond, frogs were pounded into submission mercilessly many meters from the mount without rhyme or reason. Most everywhere frogs hopped and croaked, desperate to escape the suffocating mob. Several of the thug soldiers had caught sight of Polly moving suspiciously yonder, half submerged in murky mystery. All frogs in motion, Polly made way almost to the edge of the pond now, and finally one last hop into Alara's billowed skirt, awaiting her prize.

"Wonderful! You are my treasure!" Alara stroked the frog, not thinking him so slimy now, as her champion. The front pocket to her skirt was safe harbour for Prince Polly, as Alara skipped homeward, delighted with the turn of events. Polly croaked happily at his change of fortune. What a match we have made!

Nurses and maids and tutors, gardeners and gate men and guards, the ballet, the opera, the theatre, frivolous foreign fantasies, the heart's deepest waters are stirred. A priviledged Princess and a spoilt selfish frog Prince schemed patricide, and the unification of their houses in marriage. The Prince's

pregnant political philosophy would pro-
genate a utopian empire, Polly as the wor-
shipped patriarch. But that damnded Nuck!

Hedges and lawns broke nature's advance. Alara hurried now into the domed
palace to the rings of the dinner bells. Into
the dining room she did go with imprudent
haste, startling the attention of all present.
"A miracle has occurred!", she sang sus-
pensefully, hopping three steps to Karem,
and producing her beloved in the cup of
her hands.

Grand Pooba Karem the magnificent,
exalted Magnate Supreme, poked his head
forward in shock, his eyes bulged and bog-
gled, his lips ripped bare from the teeth,
and he swung a left with panicked ferocity,
smacking the cupped hands of his darling
daughter. Prince Polly Tartakower, heir to
an empire, fired at the wall and, in a burst

of spectacular sensation, transmogrified into his naked human self.

"It's that blasted magic forest! Trolls and goblins and sprites and fairies and pixies and leprechauns and the evil of Nuck herself have worried us since time began. And now this naked frog boy!"

"Prince, I will have it known." Polly corrected his posture with pride. And dignity, I'll add. If you have been transmogrified naked you need feel no shame. Be you, and be well. But keep that thing away from me nonetheless.

Grand Pooba could see this lad was resolute, stiff as a rock, and meant what he said. Decisions such as these are puzzling for Poobas everywhere. To this Pooba the problem was thus: I can kill this man, or I can not. The Grand Pooba was suffering through the emotions attached to every possible outcome from the decision before him, when suddenly, from within the frog pocket of her frock, Princess Alara withdrew the golden bullet recovered from the pond by Prince Polly Tartakower.

An alliance was sworn to. Polly would proceed to punish and enslave yet untold millions, uninterrupted, undettered, un-yielding for eternity.

Acknowledgments

Perfect, they say, is unattainable. Probably they're right. We should, nevertheless, strive. Let's first look at the fringe fanatics that would tear society down to the studs and rebuild upon their ideals.

If, in an upheaval, you cause damage to core institutions that help our society function, then you will cause chaos. Anarchy. The removal of waste. Functioning health care services that can be deployed in a catastrophe. Supply supports demand for a whole host of goods your community requires. Do you have any idea what you're doing? Ask yourself where your water supply comes from, and how much you can depend on it? Or the type of and distribution network for your electrical supply.

Careful what services you disrupt in your petulant adolescent outrage.

For the more reasonable sort that seek change from within the institutions established, and now entrenched, by our forefathers, prepare to be disappointed. Annoyed. Frustrated. Demented with directionless rage before your day is done. One lifetime is hardly enough to change the course of the glacier that is modern law and her application. Seek, please, small measured changes that you can possibly achieve, that push in the right direction, and maybe, just maybe you'll be able to help out.

Look to the children.

Author

I've lived and I've loved and I've lost. Fate demands an immeasurable cost. What she gives out with the right is quickly taken by her left, and not in equal parts, often leaving us bereft of the means by which we seek, from our desperate situation, atrophied and weak, to alleviate the suffering descended from above. Into our grave we fear we'll fall with the slightest of fate's shove.

But hope you can, and hope you will, cause hope is life's most potent pill. Pandora, known to toy with locks, had an enigmatic box, and sure enough she opened wide the world to that from which we'd hide, the evil and the misery, Nuck's sustained artil-

lery. But with it came our last salvation, the
thread we cling to, all creation, solace in our
times of need, one last crumb on which to
feed. A feeling we can't live without, fastened
firmly, strong and stout, which all the souls
are sure to sprout, that without which we
cannot cope, our inextinguishable hope.

Meagre rations, you might say, to keep
the wolf of death at bay. Hold fast to this
last vestige from the light when trapped in
Nuck's perplexing plight. When we feel that
all is lost, beset by fate's indifferent frost,
do not let go this final rope, an fairie sent,
eternal hope.

Hell's Press

In prison does a man reside, restricted
all his days. He'll feed and groom the meat
he's in in countless futile ways. He'll tend to
psychological distress impossible to phrase.
When needs are met, he stops to think, but
just gets lost within the haze. The thoughts
are all disordered, changing, growing,
anaphase. Life, he says, is just some never
ending Cretan maze. Collapse, he does, into
a torpid, sad, life long malaise.